Lincolnshire Adventures

Edited By Sarah Olivo

First published in Great Britain in 2019 by:

 Young**Writers**®
━━━━━ Est. 1991 ━

Young Writers
Remus House
Coltsfoot Drive
Peterborough
PE2 9BF
Telephone: 01733 890066
Website: www.youngwriters.co.uk

Printed and bound in the UK by BookPrintingUK
Website: www.bookprintinguk.com
YB0413K

★ Foreword

Dear Reader,

You will never guess what I did today! Shall I tell you? Some primary school pupils wrote some diary entries and I got to read them, and they were EXCELLENT!

They wrote them in school and sent them to us here at Young Writers. We'd given their teachers some bright and funky worksheets to fill in, and some fun and fabulous (and free) resources to help spark ideas and get inspiration flowing.

And it clearly worked because WOW!! I can't believe the adventures I've been reading about. Real people, make-believe people, dogs and unicorns, even objects like pencils all feature and these diaries all have one thing in common – they are JAM-PACKED with imagination!

We live and breathe creativity here at Young Writers – it gives us life! We want to pass our love of the written word onto the next generation and what better way to do that than to celebrate their writing by publishing it in a book!

It sets their work free from homework books and notepads and puts it where it deserves to be – OUT IN THE WORLD! Each awesome author in this book should be **super proud** of themselves, and now they've got proof of their imagination, their ideas and their creativity in black and white, to look back on in years to come!

Now that I've read all these diaries, I've somehow got to pick some winners! Oh my gosh it's going to be difficult to choose, but I'm going to have SO MUCH FUN doing it!

Bye!

Sarah

Contents

Khia Scothern (10)	78
Tegan Harris (11)	80
Tianna Lisa Salt (11)	81
Jake William Harness (11)	82
Freya Khati (10)	83
Dakota Angel November (11)	84
Dawn Ball (10)	85
Jamie Arnold (11)	86
Charlie William George Gregory (11)	87
Amelia Terblanche (10)	88

Faith Hunt (10) 124

South Ferriby Primary School, South Ferriby

Abby Pickering (9)	89
Niamh Money (8)	90
Ruby Rose Davis (7)	92
Florence Mable Simons (8)	94

Waddington Redwood Primary School, Brant Road

Amelia Waller-Brown (10)	96
Fallon Bett (11)	98
Eleanor Mullins (10)	100

White's Wood Academy, Gainsborough

Caitlin Ellis (10)	102
Sophie Rickett (9)	104
Carley Warwick (11)	106
Faye Levick (10)	108
Esmé Lannigan (11)	110
Gabriella Pansy Hearn (10)	112
Katie Andrea O'Leary (11)	114
Daisy Dexter (10)	116
Hannah Louise Grimbleby (9)	118
Poppy Anderton (10)	119
Lucie Fall (9)	120
Amy Elena O'Leary (10)	121
Ella Randall (9)	122
Morgan Parks (9)	123

The Diaries

Snowy The Cat, My Cat

Dear Diary,

On Monday, it was a sunny day. Snowy, my cat, went out in the morning after his breakfast. I shouted for Snowy to come in for tea, but he didn't come in.

There was still no sign of him when I went to bed at ten o'clock. I wasn't too worried because he sometimes stayed out.

On Tuesday I called Snowy but again he didn't come back. He was on an adventure. I bet he was in the beautiful woods behind our house. He could be anywhere in there, though, because it was big for a cat. Snowy was a brave cat and he would have been excited!

On Wednesday, Snowy was still gone. I shouted for him again. I was sure he would come back that day.

Then it was night. He came back with a street dog! The street dog wasn't staying, though - he just stayed for a sleepover.

On Thursday, Snowy was back, but the dog had to go. Snowy could meet him any time.

Ella Louise Saoirse Coates (7)

Coomb Briggs Primary School, Immingham

The Winning Goal

An extract

Dear Diary,

Today was the best day of my life! It all started when my coach told me on a message that I was not on the subs bench because our main, star striker had been injured. I thought, *this could be my only chance to impress not only my teammates and manager, but also the fans for Venom Wanderers Football Club.*

Walking out of the tunnel, I could feel the atmosphere. It was tremendous! In fact, it made the hairs on the back of my neck stand up and gave me goosebumps. After shaking hands with the opposition (Red Head Rovers Football Club) it was game on.

Within the first twenty minutes, we already knew that it was not going to be easy, for they had already had several counter-attacks, countless shots and two penalties. Although it was still nil-nil at half-time, we had to have a team talk because they were dominating the match, we realised we needed to up our game.

Walking back onto the pitch was nerve-racking. I had a deep feeling inside telling me it was not going to be the game I was expecting it to be.

There were several more shots from them, but the crowd had still not seen what they were looking for. With five minutes to go, we had two shots from our team - one from a corner and one from a counter-attack. The opposition had scored but, fortunately for us, our defenders had caught them offside.

My chance had just arrived. With the ball at my winger's feet, he had gotten past a midfielder with a Maradona; we had outnumbered the defence three to two, including the goalkeeper. The ball was passed to me. With anticipation, my players were waiting for the shot...

Oakley Jon Bolland (11)

Gonerby Hill Foot CE Primary School, Gonerby Hill Foot

My Dolphin And I

Dear Diary,

My lapis-blue dolphin and I were stuck on an island and we had to live on the tiny island. The island was as big as my mother's kitchen, but my mother's kitchen sure was small! To be honest, I really didn't enjoy resting, sleeping, sitting and yawning on this little island. Obviously, neither did my pet dolphin.

"What are we going to do?" I cried. I couldn't get help because of how far away the island was from the real world.

"I don't know," my dolphin would always reply, and it never changed. I shrugged my shoulders and shook my head after hearing it - I did this every time.

One night, I just couldn't stand lying on grass and, every morning, I would have to scrape off the remaining sand in my hair. I only just noticed the poisonous water swimming around us had turned a toxic-greenish colour.

"Wake up, Dolphin!" I whispered.

Dolphin woke up and whispered furiously, "What do you want? Also, don't interrupt me in my beauty sleep ever again!"

"Look at the water!"

Dolphin looked at the toxic-greeny coloured water in surprise.

"Wow..." Dolphin began. "The colour-"

Dolphin got interrupted by me because I said, "Come on, back to sleep!"

Dolphin thought I fell asleep, but really, I didn't. I faked sleep! As soon as Dolphin saw me 'go to sleep', he fell asleep too.

I got up again and found a book near me! I picked it up like a normal person would do and saw that it was all about pandas (it was basically facts all about pandas). Before I could read it, I slowly fell asleep on the pine tree on our small island...

Sophie Neal (9)

Lincoln Gardens Primary School, Scunthorpe

The Lonely Unicorn

Dear Diary,

I feel so lonely on this part of the island when no one is around! I am so sad. I have no friends. Every part of today, I was alone, slowly eating grass on the plain part of the beautiful, special island of unicorns. All the other unicorns have gone to the enchanted part of Unicorn Island, so I am getting upset. It's just not fair, I don't like it at all! I think I will be lonely forever because no one visits this part of the mystical island. None of the other unicorns like me because of my habitat. Can you believe that? I don't know the reason. I kind of like where I live. It's quite nice, actually. I love eating the delicious long grass, it's amazing!

Dear Diary,

Today, I was galloping through the enchanted forest when I stumbled across a magical potion on the ground! It said: 'wings potion', so I tasted some which had spilt on the bumpy, rocky ground. Suddenly, I grew mystical, magical wings! They were so colourful!
Then I had an idea: I was going to fly to find friends! So I flew and flew (carefully so I wouldn't fall). Finally, I found a unicorn!

"Will you be my friend?" I asked.

"Yes! My name is Sparkles," the unicorn said.

Now we are friends and I live on the pretty side now. There are colourful, magical flowers like tulips and buttercups. Also, there are tall, enchanted trees with ripe fruits on them, like yummy apples and delicious pears! There is a flowing, glistening lake too, but the two things I really miss are the pretty flowers and the long, yummy, mouth-watering grass.

Alesha Elizabeth Kilmore (8)

Lincoln Gardens Primary School, Scunthorpe

The Monster War

9th April 3107
Dear Diary,
Yesterday, me and my dragon friends found out that there was a monster invasion! I was so scared. I went outside to run away. When I got out, I saw a monster. The war had begun. I went underwater to be safe. A sea dragon told me there were monsters down there. I went up to breathe. Everywhere I looked, there were monsters. We were surrounded...
Suddenly, they all died! My friend had done it! I flew up to shoot with my fireballs. I hit one!
"Bullseye!" I shouted.
Next, I fired a bull. I hit three million!
"Literal bullseye!" I shouted.

12th December 3110
Dear Diary,
It has been three years and a few months and the war is still going. I hope it ends soon.

12th December 3112

Dear Diary,

Only the Titan is alive now. He is badly injured, but still alive! 2,000 more hits until he's dead.
I just watched the news. The breaking news was: 'Fireball's house was destroyed'.
I said, "Oh no! I'm Fireball!" My house was destroyed by the Titan...

9th April 3114

Dear Diary,

The war has finally ended now and... we won! Hooray! My house has now been rebuilt.

10th March 3119

Dear Diary,

Everything in Dragontown has been rebuilt and I'm the president now!

Seth Michael Brooman (8)

Lincoln Gardens Primary School, Scunthorpe

The Incredible Diary Of... Godzilla

Dear Diary,

I was in New York City. I was in a bad mood, so I smashed some buildings to cheer me up. I heard a roar which I had never listened to before. Out of the shadows, a monster named MUTO rose from the water and it wasn't in a pleasing mood. My mind said, *keep trying, don't start a fight...* but before I knew it, MUTO wanted to fight!

I spoke very calmly. I was shaking. "Let's do this another day, shall we?"

MUTO accepted that we'd fight tomorrow.

The next day, MUTO was ready for a pleasant fight. My mind told me, *never give up, fight for your planet! Keep trying until he is gone.*

So I never gave in! I fought with all my might and it was time for my ultimate attack! I shot my atomic breath at MUTO, but it didn't damage him! I tried and tried. My atomic breath was nearly charged again, so I lashed him with my tail and shot my atomic breath at him again, but it didn't work! I had no clue what to do... I bit him, slashed him and whipped him with my tail, but it was just no good! How was this happening? I couldn't beat him...

I made the strongest atomic beam. It did a bit of damage, but not enough. Was this possible? Could MUTO be beaten, or was MUTO unstoppable...?

Jack Pearson (9)

Lincoln Gardens Primary School, Scunthorpe

The Daily Life Of A Cheese Ball

Six days until expiry date...

Dear Diary,

It was another day in Tesco with my cheeseball brothers and sisters just waiting to be bought. If this one guy wasn't so dumb, we could've been bought nice and early! This guy started to look at the snack aisle (the aisle we were on) for a snack. We were the only snack there, but he just left the store saying, "Meh, let's go to another store."
I mean, we were right there!

Anyway, a lady (I guess she worked at the store, since she had a nametag that said Jess) came up to the snack aisle and she actually bought us! It was so amazing that we all shed a tear.

Two days until expiry date...

Dear Diary,

I'm sorry I missed so many days, but ninety of us have been eaten and I want to congratulate them! Jess had just had her tea about two hours ago, so she ate nine of us then. I am the last one here. I hope that tomorrow, I will get eaten...

Zero days until expiry date...

Dear Diary,

Yes... I have expired and Jess never ate me. She put me in the bin first thing this morning. This is very sad. I have gone mouldy, stinky and disgusting. I will rot away. Goodbye, world...

Ryan Andrew Brannigan (10)

Lincoln Gardens Primary School, Scunthorpe

Maizy The Marvellous Child

Dear Diary,

Today, it was my first day at school in Year 3. I was so excited and I really wanted to do my best at my lessons. The only problem was that I really missed my caring, thoughtful mother.

After all of the lessons were over, I quickly walked outside and me and my friends played on the monkey bars until it was time to escape.

Finally, after five minutes, I whispered under my breath, "Quickly, it's time," and we started climbing up the black, spiky fence, hoping nobody would notice.

When we got down onto the other side of the fence, me and my friends saw five girls staring at us, so we ran as fast as we could up the straight, bumpy path. While we were walking to my house, my friends asked me, "Why are you doing this?" I said that it was because I wanted to see my mother.

Then we were at my house. I knocked on the door and I said to my mother that school had finished early because of a power cut and I wanted my friends to come over to play.

I hugged my mother and went in the back garden, but we didn't play - we climbed over the smooth brown fence and ran back to school as fast as we could... Now here I am, sat on my bed, writing my diary.

Heidi Jennifer Ling (7)

Lincoln Gardens Primary School, Scunthorpe

Teddy Teacher

Dear Diary,

Today has been the best day so far! I had three chocolate pancakes for breakfast, then I set off to school. When everyone was here, we were wondering where the teachers were.

The door handle got pushed down. The door opened! No one knew what was going on, but then a talking giant teddy turned and yelled, "I'm your teacher for today! My name is Simba. Today, we are going to be doing art!"

Everyone cheered! We started drawing whatever we wanted to until Simba put some pictures on the whiteboard and told us to draw them - so we did. He put pictures of cartoons, Pokémon and animals.

Then, after play, me and some other people were hugging Simba whilst the rest of the class were still drawing, but people who were hugging Simba had to wait because Simba needed to make a call. He did that. He came back and then the whole class heard thumps. It was a T-rex!

"Why is he here?" asked the whole class.

Simba answered this: "This is my friend! He has come to drop off chocolate eggs for you."

And that is how I had the best day so far! I wonder what's going to happen tomorrow...

Taylor Eggitt (9)

Lincoln Gardens Primary School, Scunthorpe

The Adventures Of The Moth People

Dear Diary,
It was Monday and I was staring at the big, chubby moth all night! Luckily, the human woke up to fix his submarine - we were in an underwater warehouse - but he noticed the moth and said, "Shoo! Shoo!" and mumbled, "Stupid bee."
I huffed. Then, the human started walking towards me! The moth and I fought for hours and hours and I won! Actually, none of that happened. We just fell in love and ran off into the sunset together. It was one of the best days ever!

Dear Diary,
It's Wednesday now, I've been with her (the moth) for two days now. I was wondering if I should propose. I did and she said yes!

Dear Diary,
Me and Miss Moth got married at the warehouse and had a few children. They were called Bibo, Jimmy (they were twins) and Fly Swatter Jr. The rings didn't fit that well, but that was the least of our problems.

I wanted to move to the wild west so we could be cowboys, but they wanted to stay underwater. Hopefully, all of this is a minor setback, nothing big.

PS The next day, the house was empty and a note was on the wall...

Harvey Robert Alan Jones (10)

Lincoln Gardens Primary School, Scunthorpe

Magical, Mythical Creatures

Dear Diary,

Today, I've been hanging around with my unicorn friend while getting tanned by the sun under the candyfloss tree. Then, all of a sudden, the floor started shaking. *Was it an earthquake?* I thought to myself. Then, a huge, hairy beast covered in brown, silky hair (Bigfoot) burst through the trees, bending and snapping every branch that got in the way! If you're still wondering, yes, I'm a unicorn and sorry about my writing, it's hard to write with hooves.

I'm the smartest, most intelligent unicorn in all the land and Candyland is my home. After I played with Darcie, I explored the land. I had boring adventures. I only found common creatures until I found a bridge. It looked very old. I put a hoof on the bridge and a creature I've never seen before popped up. Most unicorns called them trolls.

This troll had hairy, pointy ears and a crooked nose. I was hoping it was going to be more friendly than it looked. It's kinda sad being a unicorn because some people think that unicorns are lame and only care about rainbows, which is really sad...

Amelia Gains (9)

Lincoln Gardens Primary School, Scunthorpe

The Incredible Diary Of... Nose

Dear Diary,

I am Nose, it was my birthday yesterday. Let me tell you all about it!

I was walking in a pond on the way to my party, but then there was a smell, a smell I didn't know. The smell got stronger, stronger and stronger until I landed in a puddle of sticky, red glue! It smelled like tomato, but it wasn't... It was tomato sauce!

I was walking on grass, on the way to my party, but then there was a smell, a smell I didn't know again. The smell got stronger, stronger and stronger until I crashed into a ball, a shiny, red, plastic ball. It smelled like sugar, but it wasn't a ball... It was a cherry!

I was walking on sand, on the way to my party, but then there was a smell, a smell I didn't know again. The smell got stronger, stronger and stronger until I crashed into a pool of eels. It smelled like beef, but it wasn't eels... It was spaghetti!

I was walking over rocks on the way to my party, but then there was a smell, a smell I didn't know again. I bumped into a cake, then I realised that I was at my party!

Evangeline Mary Thompson (9)
Lincoln Gardens Primary School, Scunthorpe

The Incredible Diary Of...

Dear Diary,

I woke up in surprise. The slammed door gave me and my friends a headache. What a shock! It was Mr Burkinshaw getting ready, taking the chairs outside for a sunny day of lessons. A few hours later (I got a little more sleep), the bell rang. Oh no, another day of being swung on...

All the children came through, all the chairs being sat on one by one. It was my turn... We went through English like lightning. Break-time felt like two minutes, but maths felt like an eternity. Do you know why? Because I was outside in a bush. I don't know for how long though.

Dear Diary,

I was watching leaves rustling, hearing kids scream. I could tell it was dinnertime. At 1:15pm, someone noticed my leg. I was so relieved. I was dragged inside and cleaned until there wasn't a speck of dirt to be seen.

I had so much fun talking to my friends and knowing what happened in maths, but we did art next, so I just got covered in paint and had to be cleaned again.

That day was really hectic, so many ups and downs. I just can't explain them all to you.

Jessica Pass (10)
Lincoln Gardens Primary School, Scunthorpe

Ruby And Her Evil Robot Friend

Dear Diary,

Today, I had the most unusual day ever! I will never forget this day. It will be stored in my memories forever...

I'm a young, ten-year-old, brown-haired girl called Ruby Fearon and I have a best friend called Emily. We have been friends since we were in Year 1 or 2. We have an immense friendship - but today really shocked me.

So, I was walking around trying to find Emily, but she was nowhere to be found, not even on the tyre swing (we always play on it). But then I saw Emily walking. Emily walked up to me and grabbed my favourite glittery pencil off me. She threw it at an oak tree. I was a bit curious about why she did that, then, suddenly, she turned into an evil robot! I was so apprehensive! I screamed in fear and ran as fast as I possibly could, then I went to Miss Dweler and told her what happened. She said, "Make her drink this galaxy potion. The side effect is that she will turn the colour of a plum."

So I went to Emily. She drank the potion and she turned back to normal!
That was my day - see you tomorrow!

Emily Grace Priestley (9)

Lincoln Gardens Primary School, Scunthorpe

The Baby Dolphin

Dear Diary,

The second I awoke from my slumber, I realised what day it was... a school day! Mum shouted and told me to get ready for school. I plodded to my wardrobe, took out my school clothes and put them on. I trudged downstairs for breakfast. I had a delicious croissant, then biked to school.

I arrived and the school doors were already open. I quickly chained up my bike and sprinted inside. I got to the classroom door and walked inside. To my greatest surprise, all the tables and chairs were gone! No teacher, no friends... all that was there was a tank. I saw the slightest little splash. I cautiously walked towards the tank and realised that there, encased in the tank, was an adorable baby dolphin!

I had an amazing idea. I went outside, grabbed a rope, sprinted over to my bike, unhooked it, brought it into the playground and attached the rope to my bike frame. I picked up the tank, put it on a cart and dragged it all the way home. I put it on a cabinet in my room. Mum was fine with it. What a wonderful day it has been!

Luke Dunn (10)

Lincoln Gardens Primary School, Scunthorpe

The Unicorn Stalker

Dear Diary,

So, this is how my day went... It was early in the morning when my mum woke me up. I felt a tingle on my small, soft feet. I thought, *today is gonna be an exciting day*, so I got up, stomped to the bathroom and picked my toothbrush up out of the pot (whilst I was still half-asleep). I brushed my teeth, then I needed to get changed, so I went into my bedroom and threw on some clothes. That's when my mum shouted me down.

"Keelie, your breakfast is ready!"

I bumped down the stairs, gobbled up some breakfast and whizzed off to school.

The morning flew by. Before I knew it, it was the afternoon! As Miss Bright was teaching me, I glared out of the window and there was a beautiful, small and magical unicorn stood at the window, so I ran out of class. As I got out of class, the unicorn threw me onto its back! Before I could scream for help, it teleported me to this edible, amazing and beautiful world, but then...

My little brother woke me up! So, it was all just a dream...

Keelie Hornsby (9)

Lincoln Gardens Primary School, Scunthorpe

The Orange And Blue Twins

Tuesday,

Dear Diary,

I was in the middle of a Year 10 history exam. It was so, so boring. There were forty-five minutes left of the exam. I flipped through the book to count how many questions I had left. I had thirteen left. I got so bored, I daydreamed about lying on a hot, sunny beach.

Ten minutes passed. I stopped daydreaming. Then, I had twenty-five minutes left! I scribbled down as many answers as I could. The timer beeped. Time over. Luckily, I finished... I looked and I had two questions left! Never mind...

As I walked over to the canteen to have dinner, I got a message from my brother that said: 'My kids have been born, one blue, one orange'. I quickly ate dinner, then went to see the children. His kids were kind of random, but okay, they weren't my kids. I went back to school and the clock read 11:09pm. Bedtime!

Tomorrow would be another day...

Wednesday,

Dear Diary,

I got dressed. I had another exam today, so I went to study. Hope I get good results!

Alexandra Wrobel (10)

Lincoln Gardens Primary School, Scunthorpe

The Crazy Dinner Lady

Dear Diary,

Today was just an ordinary day - or was it? Me and my friend Chloe walked to school together. It took five minutes, but we finally arrived! It was more crowded than ever. We thought we were going to be late getting in because of the amount of people!

The first lesson of the day was with Mrs Hashtan, but people call her Mrs Hashtag, so she gets really angry. Mrs Hashtan teaches literacy. I get told off by her for just little things like writing about aliens coming in the door or not putting my things away when I am told to - little things like that get me told off.

Another two lessons before lunch passed. Now, this is the part that is unusual: it was lunchtime and a lot of people told me that a lunch lady had been speaking in a different language! It was time to get my lunch and I asked what it was, but I didn't understand a word the lunch lady said!

She left early and I just followed her. She led me to a different world, but I had to get back. I will have to go there again tomorrow...

Melissa Mai Wigham (10)

Lincoln Gardens Primary School, Scunthorpe

My Rainbow Unicorn's Diary!

An extract

Dear Diary,

Today, Ola left for school so she couldn't daydream. I could travel to Magic Land! But first, I had to get a snack. I went to Ola's room, her room is beautiful as she has tons of pictures of me. I got my snack and set off to Magic Land, I had to get there. I had to watch all the movies in the Unicorn Land cinema and I had to learn magic! It was my dream! But, I couldn't be caught.

At my age, I'm supposed to know how to use magic and I do, but there's one spell left to learn: the rainbow spell. It goes 'Rainbow, rainbow, come out to play, you haven't got all day'. Then you make a rainbow come out!

Dear Diary,

I'm in Magic Land! It's so beautiful here. My class was in twenty-five minutes and the subject is the rainbow spell! Yes! I met an alicorn, she's beautiful. Her mane is like a galaxy which has white dots for stars. Her tail is the same. She has glasses and she was heading the same way as me. Soon after that, we became friends.

Ola Aleksandra Karpinska (9)

Lincoln Gardens Primary School, Scunthorpe

Story Of Lenny The Dog

Dear Diary,

Today, my owner had their toast and went off to work. I was in the middle of my delicious, squishy breakfast when I felt a weird feeling in my tummy and I started to get stiff. I wobbled over to my basket and tried to stop the feeling.

Then I remembered that my owner was rushing off to work quickly and they forgot to change my food. They do this every day!

Eventually, I fell asleep in my basket with Bob, my teddy. When I awoke, I was really thirsty, but tired too. I walked over to my water and, because I was so sleepy, I knocked it over. Oh no! It went everywhere!

Now I was properly awake and in big trouble! I grabbed the mop as quickly as I could. I stood on my tiny, short legs and mopped while dancing. I jumped up on the oven side and grabbed the handle of the high tea towel drawer and clutched a towel and put it on the wooden floor where it was wet. Next, I jumped up and shut the drawer. After that, my owners came in and said, "Lenny, it stinks!"

Edie Holt (8)

Lincoln Gardens Primary School, Scunthorpe

Most Odd Day Ever!

Dear Diary,

Today, I had the strangest day ever! Let me tell you about it!

This morning, I woke up, jumped out of bed and threw on my uniform. I ran downstairs as fast as I could! I was so excited because I could smell the wonderful smell of waffles with maple syrup on top.

In the kitchen, I sat at the table and Mum brought my waffles through. I gobbled them up as fast as I could because the school bus would be there in five minutes. I still had to brush my teeth! I sprinted upstairs to brush them. By the time I was done, I grabbed my bag and ran outside. I got in and sat next to my best friend, Keelie.

When we got to school, we were told to sit down, when suddenly, pterodactyls came crashing through the window! However, they smelt rather nice... They were made out of chocolate! We all stood on the tables to try and catch them. As soon as I got close to catching one, they flew out the window...

Got to go now, Mum's calling me for dinner!

Clara Watson (9)

Lincoln Gardens Primary School, Scunthorpe

Fishy Frenzy

Dear Diary,

Nuke here! Today was the worst day ever. Wilson wouldn't leave me alone! Everywhere I went, he went with me. I hid under the coral, in the rock, under the gravel, but he found me in every place I hid. He is so annoying! Sometimes I wish he was gone, ugh! The only time he left me alone was when Becky dropped the food into our bowl, but the food only lasted around ten seconds because Wilson gobbled it all up!

After the food was gone, Wilson swam straight into me, so now I have bruises along my tail, my fin and my left side. They hurt. Wilson then picked up the gritty gravel with his mouth and then shot the gravel out of his mouth at me! Man, that hurt! Next, Wilson chased me around the fishbowl, but the cool coral hid me well enough for him not to find me - that was lucky! The only thing I could hear for the rest of the day was *splish splash splosh, splish splash splosh!* I need to get rid of him and I think I have a plan...

Ellie Stevens (10)

Lincoln Gardens Primary School, Scunthorpe

Alex's Diary

Dear Diary,

What an exciting day I had yesterday! It was just a normal day at school, but I overheard Sam at playtime saying, "Did you know there is a legend of a temple which, if you activate it, gives you special powers?"

After school, I asked my mum if we could go and check out the temple. She said, "Are you sure about this?"

"Yes!" I replied.

One hour of bike riding later, we got to the temple. I was confused to see a mysterious portal that was purple. I went through it, not knowing what I'd done...

I was somewhere different! I kept exploring and found the Temple of Power! I went in and saw a purple crystal. I touched it and felt weird. I was suddenly whipped back to my family...

When I got home, I noticed I had superpowers. The superpowers I got were void, ice, laser eyes, light and the power to make up my own powers!

Alexander Forrest (8)

Lincoln Gardens Primary School, Scunthorpe

The Diary Of Sheldon The Cat

Dear Diary,

Today, I was marvellous! I knocked down my next-door neighbour's million pound tray and fought the toughest cats in the world. I impressed all the girl cats as well. For breakfast this morning, I stole chicken from an old lady's kitchen and drank her dog's water. For dinner, I had fish from my cat bowl. As for tea, I had cat food. I say it's boring to my friends, but I lie - it's delicious! You have got to try it. I call myself Tough Cat, but my real name is Sheldon. No one knows I have diary apart from me - this is my super top secret diary I'm writing in right now.

Also today, I broke into a school and took all the money and said I kept it, but I really didn't - I gave it to the poor. I was kind of good today, but kind of bad too.

Also, I have a brother called Maxy. We fight a lot, but we still love each other.

Storm Stanworth (9)

Lincoln Gardens Primary School, Scunthorpe

Harry Kane's Diary

Dear Diary,

Today was a pain. We played against Man City. I feel like I've let my team down. I woke up this morning exhilarated, it was the first game. At training, we saw the 10-12s play girls vs boys. They were brilliant!

It was just fifteen minutes to the game, everybody sat there, silent. Minutes later, I shook hands with Agüero. Then, the high-pitched noise of a whistle blew. The crowd went wild, cheering me on. Dele Alli passed the ball and I scored, one-nil to us! The game carried on.

Tension scattered around the players. Half-time ended, two-one. It got worse. The whistle blew again. Five minutes into the second half and Sterling ran over me. My leg became hot and swollen. I went for an x-ray. I'm okay now and, in the end, we lost three-one! What could get any worse?

PS I'm out for the season to get better!

Ellie-Mae Howitt (10)

Lincoln Gardens Primary School, Scunthorpe

Five

Dear Diary,

Yesterday, I was bored, as usual, but then this giant said, "This will do," in a deep voice. Then, he put me in a basket, the basket was cold because it was metal. After that, this other person said, "Three pounds thirty please." I think I passed out around this time.

When I woke up, I was roasting. There was a loud noise too, *brum, brum* is what I heard. All of a sudden, it went quiet. The door opened. He got hold of me and took me through another door and launched me onto the sofa, but my number five button fell off.

Then, I went back through the doors and into the *brum, brum* thing. I was sorted again and there was a plaque that said 'Repair Shop'. He took me inside and there was another giant. Guess what? I fainted again and I had my number five button back when I woke up!

Aiden Hornsby (10)
Lincoln Gardens Primary School, Scunthorpe

Hungry Cat

Dear Diary,

My name is Bobby and I'm a cat. Today, I was talking to my brother, Percy, and he was eating a weird sandwich. I asked what it was. He said it was a peanut butter jelly sandwich. Percy told me all about it, so I was ready to try one for myself.

I walked into the kitchen. Determined, I climbed up my owner's leg and I leapt as far as I could and landed on the kitchen side. Next, I pointed at the ingredients and meowed until I got attention. My owner saw what I was doing and said, "Great idea, Bobby! I can have a peanut butter jelly sandwich for lunch!"

As he put the ingredients together, my eyes slowly glued to the delicious sandwich. As quick as a flash, I swiftly bit into the sandwich and ran away with it! This was how I had my first ever peanut butter jelly sandwich.

Write again soon!

Harley Kiddle (10)

Lincoln Gardens Primary School, Scunthorpe

The Magic Pencil

Dear Diary,

Today, I have been on a magical journey. I'll tell you what happened...

It was the worst day ever at school because I stayed in the pencil drawer where all my family live - but then, suddenly, someone threw me out of the window and broke my rubber! That's part of my head, so it really hurt!

Whilst I was out of school, I explored the school field and I found a giant brown thing. I think it was a tree. I also had heard that the most dangerous animals to a pencil or a pen are magpies because pencils and pens are really shiny and magpies are really attracted to shiny things.

Then, out of nowhere, a magpie took me and then I was snapped in half! I was bleeding out lead...

And that's what happened, the worst day ever, but at least I got to go outside and get chased around by grass monsters!

Finlay Peter May (10)

Lincoln Gardens Primary School, Scunthorpe

The Cat That Broke Into A Random Person's House

Dear Diary,

On Sunday, I broke into a random person's house (because I lived on the streets). If you're wondering how I got in, well, I just jumped through the window because the owners were too stupid to close it. I snuck in and went to the kitchen cupboards. I snuck into some cupboards to get some food, so I got all the food and realised that there were Oreos, crisps and cakes (yummy!). Now I just had to find a hiding spot. I found one under the bed, and then found a piece of paper which said that the owner had gone on holiday and was coming back at 10pm tomorrow. That was in twenty-four hours!

I decided I was just going to eat my food and go to sleep.

Dear Diary,

Oh no! The owner is coming back today. I'm going to pack up and get out of here. Bye for now!

Gabriel Costa Da Silva (10)

Lincoln Gardens Primary School, Scunthorpe

The Incredible Diary Of...
Someone Else

Dear Diary,

I didn't get much sleep last night because Ellie's rubbers threw a huge party in the case next door. Although I didn't get much sleep, I was excited because I only had one day left!

Ellie came to school and only got her ruler out. I was suspicious! I peeked out from her tray and she had an owl pencil. I was so upset!

The day went by faster than it usually did and Ellie went home. I tried to get out of this place. I got out of the window and started to walk. Someone must have picked me up when I was asleep because I ended up in a handbag that had a lot of pills in it. I had a new owner, but she passed away, so she gave me to her grandchild who was Ellie and, because I was from her grandma, she never replaced me again.

I will write again tomorrow.

Faith Borrill (10)

Lincoln Gardens Primary School, Scunthorpe

Manchester United's New Ball

Dear Diary,

I was overjoyed when Marcus Rashford made me score twice! Amazingly, it was a winning goal! At least, I thought it was. As Mohammed Salah tried to score, David de Gea (Manchester's goalkeeper) picked me up and did a pass to Rashford. Rashford booted me away, nutmegged Alisson Becker (Liverpool's goalkeeper) and scored. Manchester won, three-nil, against Liverpool FC!

After the match, I overheard Salah saying, "I can't believe Manchester United are second in the League and we are third in the Premier League!" After, I stopped listening to Mo Salah. I was in a machine that replicated footballs. Minutes later, a conveyor belt started moving and then, loads of footballs that looked exactly like me came out. I said hello but nobody answered...

Oliver Singh (9)

Lincoln Gardens Primary School, Scunthorpe

Unicorn Hurt By A Dog

Dear Diary,

It was Saturday 4th July, 2016. Maddie here and today I will write about what happened yesterday on my tenth birthday. I had a unicorn-themed party (since I love unicorns). Once my party was over, I went to Jubilee Park (which is outside my school). While I was there, I heard a puppy growling, so I followed the noise and what I saw was heartbreaking - a puppy was hurting a unicorn!

I saved the unicorn, helped it get better, fed it, watered it. My friends, Olivia, Sierra, Gracie and Madison, came over and I said, "Let's play hide-and-seek with my unicorn!"

They said, "Yes!" so I hid my unicorn. They split up to go and find my unicorn. Madison found my unicorn.

After that, I went to bed. I will write again tomorrow, bye!

Maddison Rose (10)

Lincoln Gardens Primary School, Scunthorpe

44

The Bottle

Dear Diary,

I woke up from my wooden bed and waved to the people. Someone hugged me and took me to get bought. He put me in his bag and took me to his house, then he filled me up with water.

I had my breakfast and then he took me to his school and, when he finished school, he went back home and left me at school. I waited there until the next day.

The next day, he came back and he did all his work and he took me home and I had my tea and went to bed.

The next day, I went to school with him again and he did PE and did more work. He took me home and we all had our tea and then we watched a movie together and had the best night ever. We fell asleep.

The next day, the boy didn't go to school because he was sick, so I stayed on the table all day.

Aiden Husband (9)

Lincoln Gardens Primary School, Scunthorpe

The Incredible Diary Of... A Unicorn

Dear Diary,

Yesterday, I was running wild on a field. At midday, two humans came. I stood as still as a statue. I didn't know what was going on. I wanted to run, but I thought it would be a bit rude. Then, I couldn't keep quiet any longer, so I spoke. The tall human didn't say a word until the little human said, "Can I have her? She's lovely!"

Me and my new friends went to a place they called 'home' and watched a screen. I didn't know what it was. I thought we could see moving people. The little human put me on the screen. I felt excitement running through my body. I just wanted to scream. I was so excited to have human friends. When the humans left, I kept screaming with excitement.

Darcie Leaning (9)

Lincoln Gardens Primary School, Scunthorpe

The Death Of Iron Man

Saturday 13th May, 1989
Dear Diary,
Captain America here! Earlier, Iron Man went to the market with Max the dog. They were getting food, but Max and Iron Man got blown up by a grenade launcher! The spiky-haired man with the grenade launcher was laughing.
An ambulance came for Iron Man, but he was dead already...

Sunday 14th May, 1989
Dear Diary,
Yesterday, Iron Man died, so today was his funeral. All the Avengers cried for Iron Man. We planned a revenge plan and we will get revenge soon for Iron Man.

Tuesday 16th May, 1989
Dear Diary,
Today, we got revenge on Spiky-Haired Man.
Boom! Bang! Crash! Bang!
Now we can sit down and relax for the rest of the day!

Lily Stevens (10)
Lincoln Gardens Primary School, Scunthorpe

A Dog That Goes To School

Dear Diary,

One school day, I got ready for the first day of Year 5. I walked to school at 7:35 so I got there on time. I was very scared of going to school for the first day, but I knew I would do work and have fun lessons, then I would get dinnertime and play time. I went home at 3:15. I love hometime! I'll write again.

Dear Diary,

Today, I got up for school and I got ready and had some breakfast. Next, I went off to school with my best friend, Jasper the cat. I am going to do maths first. I love doing multiplying by ten.

Me and Jasper went to play in the playground after the maths lesson. We played tig and cops and robbers, our favourite games.

I'll write again soon!

Liam Darren Good (10)

Lincoln Gardens Primary School, Scunthorpe

The Incredible Diary Of... Freddie Mercury

Dear Diary,

Mercury here! Today was my biggest show ever. It was amazing! I'll tell you all about it.

It all started when I arrived there. I was nervous at first. I took a deep breath. I closed my eyes. I heard the curtain open. I walked out first. I heard cheers for my name. Everything was going fine until I walked over to the piano and I slipped. Everyone was laughing at me, but I got up and acted like nothing happened. I walked over to my piano and it sounded weird. The crowd booed and threw stuff at me and started to leave.

I tuned my piano and played. I saw people sing and dance. The arena filled up again! When I arrived home, it was about 2am.

That's all! Speak to you tomorrow!

Kaydan Seaman (10)
Lincoln Gardens Primary School, Scunthorpe

The Incredible Diary Of...

Dear Diary,

Today has been one of the most worrying days of my life. My three most loved pugs were kidnapped last night...

I came down at 7:30am and I couldn't hear my pugs. I found that very strange since they normally would come running in whilst barking like crazy. However, this time, they didn't, so I went into the kitchen and they weren't in there, so I had to go on a mission to find my missing pugs.

I quickly dashed up the stairs and then I saw a note on my wardrobe which said: 'I have taken your pugs so I can meet you in person. It's okay because they're in good hands. For the first clue, head to Big Ben. See you soon...'

George Caris (8)
Lincoln Gardens Primary School, Scunthorpe

Leave Me Alone!

Dear Diary,

I was back at work again when this girl got her dripping, sweating hand around my whole, entire body, strangling me just like I was a cat. *Here we go again...* I thought. She was tapping me on the table, giving me a huge headache! She even likes to chew me and throw me across the table - just imagine if that was you!

I had a plan which I will share with you: I decided I was going to go and hide in the drawer with my friends. She saw me close the drawer. I thought to myself, *oh no! She's going to find me! Wish me luck...*

I could hear her footsteps. Luckily, she picked up the pencil next to me...

Write again tomorrow!

Ellie Hope (10)

Lincoln Gardens Primary School, Scunthorpe

The Magic Football

Dear Diary,

On Tuesday, in the Champions League, I found myself in a locker with all my ball friends. Suddenly, they picked me as the Champions League ball. Suddenly, I was kicked over the stadium. I was lost and frightened.

I was popped! I couldn't believe it! The dog's teeth looked like white, pointy daggers. I was so flat, there was not a particle of air in me. It was the worst thing that ever happened to me.

Luckily, I was found. It was a miracle. The boy put a plaster on me and pumped me up. I was fixed and he took me back to Old Trafford, then I scored three goals! I was so happy to be back with all my ball friends.

Lewis Ferguson (10)

Lincoln Gardens Primary School, Scunthorpe

The Billionaire

Dear Diary,

Today, my mum won the lottery and made my life better than ever! Now I have a mansion! I'm a princess and I met the queen. I have four swimming pools. I have servents and a butler and a Chihuahua (actually, lots of them!). My brother is John Cena (the wrestler) - awesome!

"Royalty is cool!" I said. I called my Chihuahuas for dinner. "Rosey and Rosette! Din-dins!"

But I nearly got destroyed - they jumped on me! I had so many Chihuahuas that they actually filled the mansion.

"Argh!" I screamed. It was hopeless with so many Chihuahuas licking me like mad! I wish I was them!

Bethany Pattinson (9)

Lincoln Gardens Primary School, Scunthorpe

The Incredible Diary Of...

Dear Diary,

I was running around in the garden, playing with my squeaky toy. I always caused mischief, day and night. I was at home playing mischievously. Suddenly, my squeaky toy went missing, so I went to find it. Soon, it would be night so I headed home. I was soon in my cosy bed for bedtime. Suddenly, I found my toy, it appeared to be under the shed.

Dear Diary,

Today was the best day of my life, I did something brave today. I made friends with another dog. We played together and we went to my house to play, then he went home. I was nervous like a sad raincloud when it rained. I was a really good dog today.

Mia Marshall (9)

Lincoln Gardens Primary School, Scunthorpe

Winning Wembley

Dear Diary,

I walked out of the tunnel to prepare for what was coming at me. My spine tingled and my teammates vomited on the way out. The crowd did a mix of cheers and boos as we walked onto the emerald green pitch.

Ninety minutes had gone and it was one-one. We had extra time, but it was still a draw, so it went to penalties. The first penalty was taken and it went in. A few shots later, it was three-two to us, but they got the next penalty. He walloped it at raging speed, but I saved it. The crowd cheered and I celebrated. I won Wembley, it was so incredible, I couldn't believe it!

Adam David Fairweather (10)

Lincoln Gardens Primary School, Scunthorpe

The Incredible Diary Of...

Dear Diary,

The day had passed, I was hit in the face so many times, I couldn't remember what the score was after the game. My hands were swollen from getting hit by the power of the players. After a while, the storm started to come onto the pitch as the nets started to blow and the players and I were getting worried.

As soon as the storm started to come in, I ripped and an Old Trafford fan's arm broke when the net ripped. As the Old Trafford fans cried out with tears and as soon as the kid was hurt, the game was called off and the kid went to hospital.

Thomas Ross (9)

Lincoln Gardens Primary School, Scunthorpe

Mind City

Dear Diary,

You would never believe the day I've had!

It all started like this... When I was playing Minecraft in my bedroom, the screen suddenly went black and purple and it sucked me into the TV! My character was frozen, so I got all my tools and went mining to get some iron.

I had been mining for hours and hours when I ran into diamond - a lot of it! I got at least sixty-four diamonds. I ran back to the top and saw a portal, so I ran through. I was back at home...

I will write again soon. Goodbye!

Bradley Kirkby (8)
Lincoln Gardens Primary School, Scunthorpe

SpongeBob's Greatest Day (Kind Of)

Dear Diary,

Today, I went jellyfishing with Patrick. It was fun! Even Squidward went!

Well, I had to go to work with Squidward at 1pm, so, kindly, Squidward offered me a ride on the back of his boat. Tied on by string, we set off at 12:30pm, but something disastrous happened: the string snapped! Ugh!

We walked inside. I won 'employee of the month'! I went home to show Gary, but Patrick had eaten my house! What do I do now?

Speak to ya tomorrow, Diary.

Alesha Peebles (10)

Lincoln Gardens Primary School, Scunthorpe

The Best Friend Spies

Dear Diary,

I went to Dillen's house and we heard that there was a robbery at a bank! Me and Dillen are secret agents, so we went to see what happened. We asked the policeman what happened. The policeman told us.

Me and Dillen found the thief and he went to prison but he escaped! We looked for him and he was robbing another bank. We caught him again!

Miky-Robert Junior Edon (9)

Lincoln Gardens Primary School, Scunthorpe

Spectacular Shopping Spree

Dear Diary,

I was stood in the midst of America! We arrived in New York City, 17/02/18, 11:57am. We stayed for three days! On our last day, we went on a shopping spree so we could buy what our hearts desired! I was given $300 and spent £158.63 on that day in one and a half hours!

But life cannot be perfect and karma needs to do her job, so I had two rude-ish shopping experiences. I'll explain one - and only one!

We went to my holy grail, Victoria's Secret, and I practically bathed in all the products. I had over five shopping bags of Victoria's Secret, all different products (undergarments, sportswear, cosmetics, new lip regime products, etc.). I arrived at the colossal line of forty-two people. I was there for a tedious thirty minutes.

As I finally approached the front of the line, I walked towards the till and took out my Louboutin purse and the male employee looked me up and down, thinking, *Why has she got expensive items? Spoiled brat.* Seconds later, he spoke into his microphone and said, "I'll go on my forty-five minute break now," and stormed off!

I was irate, but it didn't phase me. I was sophisticated and tranquil, so I sauntered off to another till and placed down my items, but that lady wasn't having it. Her annoying, middle-aged self told me, "Sweetie, you have to wait in line," in her silly American accent! I was livid. Steam was coming out of my ears, so I stormed off, furious but confident, and spent money on retail therapy. I came back to get loads more and spent another $200-$300 with Mum and family.

Nia Praise Vongai Charehwatenda (10)

National Junior School, Castlegate

Haunted House Fail!

Dear Diary,

It was a long journey to London, but we finally made it! We were going to Winter Wonderland. There were rides everywhere and, of course, I wanted to go on them! My mum was very kind and gave me £50 to spend there - but, of course, that was a bad idea, because if I had money, it would be gone in five minutes! Of course, it was very busy there. People were pushing and shoving, which annoyed me, but overall, I was having a good time. The great thing was that there were lots of food places. I went with my mum, sister, my mum's friend and her two daughters. You know... them people.

The first thing we did was go ice skating. I'm not that bad at ice skating but, weirdly, I was that day. We went to some other places, but, you know... that was boring. We went to an ice kingdom, which was -15° (freezing!), but I guess it was cool.

Here comes the funny part: it was around 9:35 at night. We were walking around the area and we saw a haunted house which was also a roller coaster ride.

Obviously, I wanted to go on it, but, unfortunately, the line was too big and, to be honest, I couldn't be bothered to wait - so I didn't! There was a bench next to it with a scary, zombie-like statue sat on the bench. Obviously, my mum wanted me to sit next to it to get a photo (like all mums do) so I sat down. As I sat next to it, my mum was about to get a photo. Just as she clicked the button, the statue spat water at my face - disgusting! We then walked away, laughing our heads off. What an embarrassing moment!

Brody Erica Hansom (11)
National Junior School, Castlegate

Road Trip

Dear Diary,

You will not believe what happened today! Usually, I would just be in my bed sleeping, but this morning, Mum had another out-of-nowhere plan for me. She said to me, "We are going on a road trip!"

I asked her to get out of my room so I could get changed. After I went downstairs, there was juice spilt on the side and there was drool from the dog, so what did Mum do? She shouted to me, "Can you clean all of that up before we go?"

So... I started with the juice because it was dripping onto the floor. When that was out of the way, I started to clean up the drool.

I heard outside, *beep, beep!* I heard the car starting up, so I had to leave the drool and jump into the car.

We started to drive. Mum didn't tell me where we were going. We were on the highway. I said to her, "Where are we going?"

She said, "You will find out!"

It left me curious for a while.

Suddenly, I saw black smoke coming out the back of the car! It started to slow down.

I said to Mum, "What's happened?"

She said, "The car's broken down."

We got out and saw a lot of smoke - it was like a campfire. I shouted, "Oh my god, we're gonna blow up!"

Mum said, "Be quiet." She started the car back up.

"We're safe!" I screamed.

Then we drove off into the distance in the tin can Mum calls a car.

Jack Kilgallon (11)
National Junior School, Castlegate

The Trip To Disneyland

Dear Diary,

Normally I would wake up around 8am, but today, Mum woke me up at 6am and she said she had a surprise for me. Mum didn't usually have surprises for me and, if she did have surprises, they weren't the best. I went downstairs to get my breakfast and in the hallway were some suitcases. We hadn't been on holiday for a while and I had no clue where we would be going.

I was *very* surprised when Mum told me that we were going to Disneyland! We'd never been to Disneyland before and everyone at school was always saying how fun it was. We got in the car and headed to the train station. I asked Mum why we couldn't just go on an aeroplane. She said it was because Disneyland is in France, so there'd be no point in us going on a plane.

We were on the train for four hours and when we got to the hotel it took ages to sign in. I asked Mum if we could at least go on one ride and she said yes, but it had to be quick.

There was one ride that I really wanted to go on called Space Mountain. It was a roller coaster and I was just the right height! When we sat down, ready to take off, I realised that it was in a tunnel! We took off and we were going so fast that I couldn't see anything.

Nobody told me that there was a camera that took pictures, so at the end, my face wasn't the best!

Ali Jorja Cockerton (11)
National Junior School, Castlegate

The Stairs Disaster!

Dear Diary,

Normally, I have a long nap after breakfast for a while, but today, Dad had other plans. He decided that I, the most sporty person in the family, did not do enough sports! This, coming from the person who hasn't done any sports in the last three years! So yeah, he decided that me and him were going to sign up for golf club! I asked why Kian wasn't going to sign up as well and Dad responded with this: "Because he already does enough sports!" Now *that* was annoying, because Kian always refuses to do *any* sports whatsoever!

Then Dad said, "Your brother plays in the sun every day and gets all the vitamin D he needs and you don't even go outside!"

I tell Dad that I get enough vitamin D from my video games, but for some reason, that never seems to work on him.

So me and him went to our rooms to get dressed and we only got to go after Dad eventually chose which shoes he was gonna wear. I mean, how long does it take for a man to choose his shoes? We started to walk down the stairs, but dad fell! He did a somersault onto his butt! I laughed my head off and the first thing I did was send a picture to my friends and tell them what happened.

I was ecstatic! That was the end of the idea to sign me up to stupid golf club - for now and hopefully ever...

Owen George Vickers (11)

National Junior School, Castlegate

Holiday Harrassment

Dear Diary,

Never have I ever been on such a pathetic holiday! I didn't even have a bloomin' bed! And the worst part: the hotel looked *nothing* like the one in the photos. It's what my nerdy brother would call a scam. I never wanted to go on holiday - I don't know why us kids are forced to go where our parents tell us to. My dad is a smart guy, but sometimes I wonder what goes on in his head. Mum said that, if we couldn't relax inside, then we'd better just go outside. The temperature outside was freezing, but Mum wasn't having it. She said the cold was going to 'bring us together as a family'. I'm pretty sure she was imagining one of those magical family holidays where everyone had an enjoyable time and 'came together'. Well, that wasn't going to happen, but Dad said I was just being pessimistic. Magazines are expectations, my life is reality. If we'd just stayed home, none of this would've happened.

The night was even worse! I had to sleep in the same bed as my useless brother. Well, I had to *try* to sleep. This is why us lads need our own rooms.

Anyway, that's how I ended up dragging a blanket and a pillow to the bathtub, but I had to try to avoid the black mould! Looked like I still wasn't gonna get any sleep...

Rania Ali (11)
National Junior School, Castlegate

Crispy Chip Crisis

Dear Diary,

You won't believe what happened to me today!

Well, my mum was in the kitchen as usual, cooking while I was lying on the sofa watching YouTube, but my sister had other plans; she wanted to just annoy me! After a while, my sister was making me really angry!

I could smell something. I wondered what it was... probably just my mum cooking still. But then there was smoke coming out of the kitchen! I thought it was probably just whatever my mum was cooking, so instead of freaking out, I watched some pug videos.

But then, *beep, beep!* The fire alarm!

Mum ran in and said, "Quickly, fire!"

I risked my life for my iPad. My dog jumped over us all to make it outside - he wasn't waiting for us to come!

When it was over, my mum told us, "It's okay now," and I was saying the same to my iPad.

After that, I was pretty stressed and the best thing for stress is food, but our chips were burnt! My dad said, "They're only slightly burnt," but they weren't. They were ashes.

I went upstairs to check on my hamster. My cat Sid was just asleep! He slept through it! My dog was barking, my sister was moaning... what a hectic day!
Now it's time for bed. I hope it doesn't happen again!

Josh Eric Matsell (10)
National Junior School, Castlegate

The Worst Day Ever!

Dear Diary,

In the afternoon, we were driving to Belvoir Castle to watch the fireworks, which cost my dad £36. It looked a beautiful day to go there, but as for me, I found it boring because we'd seen fireworks before, so what was the point of going there? My dad said that these fireworks were big and awesome.

When we arrived there, it felt like it took two hours to walk to the field - then we had to go to the toilet and he said, "Hurry up!" like he was the boss. It took ten minutes to go to the toilet! When I went to the toilet, I forgot to lock the door and a man came into my toilet and screamed! It was embarrassing and there could've been a cameraman taking a video of me. I thought my life was over.

As it was getting dark, the fireworks began. We sat on the grass. It started chucking rain and we had no umbrella, just our coats!

I said, "Can we go home?"

My dad said no, because he said it would stop. But it didn't. One person gave us some doughnuts, which was nice, but most of my clothes were wet, so we decided to go home.

Whilst we were running to the car, my shoes were soaking wet! Really, this was the worst day ever; getting wet, watching boring fireworks and not getting prepared for the day!

Jayan Panchal (11)

National Junior School, Castlegate

The Wonderful World Of Bobsilia Bob!

Dear Diary,

Today was one of the best days of my life. You will never believe what happened...

It started off as a normal day (well, it wasn't a fully normal day because it was Christmas) and me and my family woke up nice and early, which for me is a record as I normally roll out of bed at 10:30am. Today, I wanted to get up at 6am to open my presents.

After that, my family came round for dinner, and here's where our story begins...

My house was full of people - aunts, uncles, grandmas, grandads, brothers, sisters, mums and dads - but none of us were allowed in the kitchen, as Mum said that's where all the magic happened. Well, something happened in there, but I wouldn't call it magic!

"Argh!" screamed Mum! A ginormous *crash, bang, wallop* came from the kitchen. We all ran in there. Turned out Mum had forgotten the oven was on and put the parsnips (which were in a glass pot) on top of it. It had exploded! When Mum tried to clean it up, the parsnips burnt through the dustpan and grease went everywhere - but the funniest thing was that Mum got stuck in splits on the floor.

None of us helped her - we were too busy laughing!

Phenix Bowen-Higgs (11)
National Junior School, Castlegate

Sleepover Drama

Dear Diary,

Today was the most embarrassing day of my life! I was so excited because I was going to my friend's house for a sleepover. I got all of my stuff ready and my dad was on the way to take me. I could not wait! I could hear knocking at the door. I ran downstairs and my dad was there, so I got my stuff.

Five minutes later, I was at her door, about to knock. I knocked. Her name is Mia. She answered the door. She shouted, "Khia!" and I shouted, "Mia!" She said, "Come in!"

We went upstairs to put my stuff away in her room. We were lying on the bed playing Fortnite. We played for about an hour, but we got bored, so Mia showed me her special unicorn blanket. You could put your feet in it. I had a go, then Mia dared me to stand up in it, so I did.

Mia showed me her cheerleading dance and I was turning around, but I forgot I was still in the unicorn blanket and I tripped over my feet and fell on my back, but I didn't hurt myself. I was laughing and then Mia asked if I was okay. I was fine!

We got into our PJs and went on our phones, then we were really tired so we went to sleep.

Khia Scothern (10)

National Junior School, Castlegate

Wrong Car! Oops!

Dear Diary,

It was a warm summer's day when me and my sister were walking to Lidl's car park to meet my mum. I went ahead of my sister and ran to my mum's car. I pulled a funny face through the window. I got inside and put my seatbelt on, then chucked my bag on the back seat.

But I kept looking around the car and there were loads of unusual things that I knew we didn't have. I looked in the driver's seat and realised it wasn't my mum. Oops! That was very embarrassing!

I quickly got my bag from the back, jumped out of the car and said to the driver, "Sorry, wrong car!" and slammed the door as I was so embarrassed! I ran away. My sister was laughing loads.

After that, I went to the right car, then I waited 'til my mum's friend had gone before I told her the story. I told her what happened, then she laughed her head off!

We decided to leave the car park. I noticed that the car I accidentally got into was the same make and colour as ours. As we left, we saw the car that I accidentally went into and they stared at me!

Tegan Harris (11)

National Junior School, Castlegate

The Day My Cat Fell Into The...

Dear Diary,

It was April 25th, 2018 when I was eating my breakfast (like a normal person), but obviously my cat knew because she came padding up to me (very slowly) and then stared straight into my eyes! Now, usually this would be normal for my cat, but the way she was looking at me gave me shivers down my back. I knew she was up to something...

So, normally if my cat wanted to get up to the breakfast bar, she would need to jump onto the bin, but today, my mum had taken the bin lid off ready to clean the bin out, but Candy didn't know this... so she pounced up onto the bin and instead fell inside! As I was laughing (almost in tears) my mum shouted, "Candy! Now we will have to give you a B-A-T-H."

Now, I don't know if Candy understands human English, but as my mum said that final 'H', candy began to go crazy and tried to jump out of the bin! From that day on, Candy has always used the dining table to get onto the breakfast bar and has never gone near the bin again...

Tianna Lisa Salt (11)

National Junior School, Castlegate

Pets

An extract

Dear Diary,
Actually getting up at weekends is the worst! From the moment Mum pulled open the curtains today and announced that it was going to be a good day, I knew it was gonna be the exact opposite. My first priority, of course, was to get dressed and then go downstairs to feed the hamster and the goldfish (aka Nippy and Nemo). The goldfish were easy to feed - however, the hamster proved to be a bit more of a challenge. As soon as I put the food into his bowl, he came to greet it. At least, that's what I thought he was doing. In fact, he leapt off the ground like some sort of ninja rodent and bit the end of my finger! I quickly withdrew my finger, but guess what? He was hanging onto it with his teeth! I frantically shook my finger about, trying to get him off, and I eventually succeeded... however, there was blood coming from my fatal wound and I was sure that I would be scarred for life. I hope you can guess which of my pets is Nippy and which one is Nemo!

Jake William Harness (11)
National Junior School, Castlegate

Chair Trouble

Dear Diary,

I don't like chairs. I don't like them at all. Why? Well, it all began a few years ago...

It was a typical summer day. I was at a friend's house and we were bored, so we went to the den and decided to play truth or dare. When it was finally my turn, my friend dared me to put my head in-between a chair's seat and back or to eat a mouldy orange!

I did the most reasonable thing and put my head in the chair, but when I tried to get out, my ears got in the way! My ears betrayed me! I was stuck...

I didn't want to tell my parents 'cause they would laugh, so I screamed, "Argh!"

My friend's dog got excited after I screamed and jumped onto the chair, tipping it over!

I was stuck like this for what seemed like forever, but when my mum came, she just turned my head and it slipped out! What? Unbelievable!

Freya Khati (10)
National Junior School, Castlegate

A Slippery Disaster

Dear Diary,

It started off a perfectly normal, chilly, wintry morning. I was getting ready for school (boring!). I was putting on some warm clothes, doing my hair, brushing my teeth, having something really *not* healthy for breakfast, but Mum stopped me right there. She had other plans for me. She made me a nutritious breakfast.

After I had my breakfast, I was about ready to go to school, so me, my brother, mum and dad headed out the front door. I said goodbye to my dad as my mum was taking us to school. I was gonna get in the car, but I needed to be careful; it was really icy on the ground, until... *thud!* My dad had slipped over and fallen on the floor! We had to see if he was okay before we burst out with laughter.

After a while, we got over it and headed on to school in our tin can that my mum calls a car.

Dakota Angel November (11)

National Junior School, Castlegate

The Hitting Sister

Dear Diary,

On Friday 8th March, my stepdad got me and my sister a wooden sword and shield each. We started fighting, then, within about ten seconds of having them, I hit my sister in the face with my sword. All of us started giggling (me, my mum, my stepdad and my sister, Sarah). Next time, I tried not to hit her in the face.

Two days later, my stepdad was fighting Sarah. My stepdad went to hit her. She tried to block it, but she hit herself in the face with her own shield! I started laughing and giggling. It was really funny! My sister cried a bit, but she was fine after.

Now I know not to fight my sister again unless she asks me to fight her! We are okay now.

Dawn Ball (10)
National Junior School, Castlegate

The Runaway Dog

Dear Diary,

Today was the first day of summer holidays, so I planned to play on my computer, but Mum had other ideas. Yeah, that's right - I had to walk the dog! I begged her to let me stay home, but there was no changing her mind, so I put the dog on the lead and we headed out.

We finally arrived at the field. There were hundreds of people there. The dog caught me off guard and took me far away from my mum. She called my dog so he went running back, pulling me over and dragging me across the grass. Everyone was watching and laughing their heads off!

Jamie Arnold (11)

National Junior School, Castlegate

The Diary Of Charlie's Weekend

Dear Diary,

Last weekend, I went outside to play some tennis with my sister and, as I was playing, I went to get the ball, but a pole was in the way! I tripped up and hurt my leg. As I got up, my sister laughed her head off.

When my mum came out, she said, "What happened?"

I said, "I am okay, I tripped on a pole."

Mum did the same!

I went in and watched a film and put my feet up, and that was the end of my weekend.

Charlie William George Gregory (11)

National Junior School, Castlegate

The Pool Fall Over

Dear Diary,

I thought I was just going to have a lazy day, but my mum had other plans. I had to go to my aunty's house! I had food there and it was disgusting!

In the afternoon, me and my cousin went outside and played football (my cousin's version of it). As I was playing around, I did a handstand next to the pool.

Then, twenty minutes later, I was stood waiting for my mum - then my stupid cousin decided to shove me in the pool!

Amelia Terblanche (10)

National Junior School, Castlegate

Worst Day Ever

Dear Diary,

The worst day ever! When I woke up, I got out of my bed and tripped over my rug onto my bookcase, which fell on me. I got up out of the pile of books and walked into the kitchen. I then tripped over the dog and got a face full of cream cheese! Finally, after I washed my face, we got in the car to go to school. I forgot it was sports day, so I didn't have my PE kit and I had to play in my underwear!

After sports day was over, I went into the bathroom and somehow got my head stuck in the toilet! Then, in my science class, I added the blue liquid to the pink liquid and it exploded! It was hometime and my family and I were going out to tea. After our meal, it was time for dessert. However, I stood up and knocked the desserts out of the waiter's hands, which all landed - yes, you guessed it - on my head!

When we got home, I rushed into my bedroom and locked the door!

Abby Pickering (9)
South Ferriby Primary School, South Ferriby

The Incredible Diary Of... Isla The Ice Skater

Dear Diary,

Today was my skating competition. It was the most scary day of my life!

I woke up this morning with goosebumps and butterflies in my stomach. I felt like I was going to crumble like cookie crumbs.

When we arrived at the skating rink, we went to the locker room so that I could get changed and put away my things. Mum chatted to my coach as I did my stretches when, suddenly, I felt someone push me to the ground!

I quickly jumped up and turned around to see who had shoved me and I saw two mean-looking girls laughing at me. The girls skipped away when they noticed the coach walking towards us.

"Don't worry about those girls - just concentrate on your performance!"

I felt butterflies, so I quickly ran to the toilet. When I got back, I spotted something... my ice skates had disappeared! I scuttled to my mum and tried to tell her what happened.

"They've stolen my skates!" I sobbed.

When I looked up, I saw my coach walking towards me with my skates in her hand.

"Thank you!" I sighed with relief.

"Quickly, put them on! It's time for your performance."

As I got onto the ice, the butterflies disappeared and I felt confident - then I skated the best I have ever skated in my whole life! I won first prize. As I collected my trophy, I could see the mean girls looking at me, so I gave them a cheeky smile!

Niamh Money (8)

South Ferriby Primary School, South Ferriby

The Incredible Diary Of... Cooper The Cat

Dear Diary,

This morning when I woke up, the sun was shining, so I decided to let my cat, Cooper, play outside. He was taking a while outside, which was unusual for him to do. A couple of minutes later, my friend Tracy rang me to say that my cat, Cooper, was stuck up a tree beside a pond in the park. So, I got changed and put my shoes on and ran outside the front door as fast as I could to the park.

When I arrived, I could see lots of people gathered around the tree that Cooper was stuck up. He looked frightened and was meowing very loudly. I wondered how on earth he got up there! I asked my friend Tracy. She said that she saw him chasing some little birds playfully near a pond. The birds had flown up the tree to their nest for protection. However, Cooper decided to follow and that is how he got stuck up the tree.

I decided to call the fire brigade to help. When they arrived in the big red fire engine, they grabbed some big ladders and climbed up them to help Cooper. Cooper looked at them, scared and confused, then he decided to run up the tree more!

The firemen shouted, "It's okay, Cooper! I'm here to help you!"

Cooper saw how friendly the fireman was and walked carefully back to the fireman's arms. The fireman gave me Cooper and I took him home. Now he just watches the birds playing from inside the house through the window, safe and sound.

Ruby Rose Davis (7)
South Ferriby Primary School, South Ferriby

Winter Wind

Dear Diary,

Today, I have had the greatest day of my life! It all started on a cold, frosty morning when I was going to collect firewood for my family. While I was collecting wood, one stick caught my eye. It had little sprinkles of white fairy dust on it. I thought I'd better take a look, but when I touched it, it pricked me. I was surprised that it had prickles. I felt a little twinkle on my nose, then, suddenly, I felt a rush of cold through my body like an electric shock! It made me feel dizzy and woozy for a few moments until I came round.

When I did come around, I had superpowers! How did I know I had superpowers? Well, I didn't know until I touched the frosty stick again and the weather changed from frosty, crisp and cold to a bubble of bright, hot sunshine that melted all of the frost and little specks of snow away. The flowers bloomed and birds sang around me, but only in the wood - everywhere else was still frozen. I quickly realised that the stick was magic, and with it, I could change the weather around me. I ran home and hid the stick under my bed.

What a day it had been! I was still in shock and scared, but so excited about what the future would bring...

Florence Mable Simons (8)

South Ferriby Primary School, South Ferriby

The Incredible Diary Of... Sherly Holmes, Sherlock Holmes' Daughter

Dear Diary,

Today, I woke up and felt a slight pain in my chest. For a second, I was worried about it, but then ignored it. As I made my way downstairs, I couldn't hear Dad's morning piano - he was on a business trip again. I went downstairs and saw that Mum wasn't in her pinstripe suit.

"Morning, Mum," I said in a wondrous tone.

"What...?" she said sleepily. "Oh! Morning, hun."

"Why aren't you in your work outfit?" I asked.

"Day off," she muttered.

I was getting nervous. Mum *never* takes days off, so why today? Mum looked anxious.

"Sweetie, um..." she pondered. "Dad had an accident last night and is in hospital as we speak. He might not be home for a few weeks."

My dad is Sherlock Holmes, protector of London!

"Who will save London now?" I inquired nervously.

"If a superhero pops up and just so happens to save the day, then yes - but if not, then no one. Sorry, sweetie," she said as she kissed me on the forehead.

I went back to my room, slammed my door, sat on my bed and thought, *can this day get any worse?* But an idea popped into my head from what my mother said: 'if a superhero pops up'... I could pop up, save the day and save London! But I needed a sidekick...

I called my friend Liz and she agreed to be my sidekick. Now I had a city to save, but I still needed a name...

I stuck to my old one: Sherly Holmes.

Amelia Waller-Brown (10)
Waddington Redwood Primary School, Brant Road

Gary's Great Adventure!

Dear Diary,

Today was crazy! I've never experienced something so strange in my life! I'd heard stories about pickles that ventured out into the beyond, or who were 'chosen' only to never come back, but those were stories old Grandma Gherkin used to tell me when I was barely the size of a pea.

Anyway, it was a normal Tuesday and I was sat in my jar, floating around and watching the world go by, when all of a sudden, a strange creature appeared and made their way across the kitchen towards my jar.

Well, that's odd, I thought.

Suddenly, the creature reached for the lid. I was in awe once she actually opened the pickle jar (normally even adults can't do it). Oh no... she couldn't pick me! I had so much to do today! I had to feed Pip the cat, eat ice cream, go for a walk and so much more!

In the blink of an eye, her little fingers latched onto me. This was it. This was the end! She crunched and crunched, then darkness. I had blacked out...

As soon as I woke up, I noticed something strange about myself... I was a poo! This couldn't be! I am all horrible and squishy! Right now, I am still speeding down a long tube into the abyss.

Not sure where I'll stop, not sure when I'll stop, but tomorrow is a new day.
Until then,
Gary the pickle.

Fallon Bett (11)
Waddington Redwood Primary School, Brant Road

The Crash!

Dear Diary,

Today, something extraordinary happened, but it wasn't positive as I was seriously injured in the event...

Thankfully, school was over. I wandered closer and closer to a black car which looked brown. Mum joyfully exclaimed, "How was school, Hunny Bun?" I gave no verbal answer, just a groan of rage.

As soon as we drove off, a red lorry drove in our direction. We were only fifty metres from my school entrance when the crash happened...

My teachers (Mr Pottes, Miss Uddin, Mrs Woodrey, Mr Taylor and Miss Costello) came sprinting to the crash site. Someone anonymous dialled 999 (thank you, whoever you are). I had billions of goosebumps covering my puny arms and legs, my heart came first in a running race and I was half unconscious...

Now I'm at hospital. I have not got a clue how I was transported here. My annoying sister, Daisy, and my two best friends, Josh and Luke, came to see me.

I am so lucky to have friends and teachers like them. Furthermore, I am so grateful for what everyone has done for me.
More tomorrow,
Sam Luis Helbick.

Eleanor Mullins (10)
Waddington Redwood Primary School, Brant Road

The Unexpected School Visit

An extract

Dear Diary,

What a day! Aliens took over the whole school. It started at school where I was answering a difficult division equation. Esmé was talking to me about my favourite book 'The Hunger Games'. But, I wasn't listening. I saw a disk-shaped hovercraft getting closer and closer. Then, I heard a loud whirr.

When we looked outside, we all saw the hovercraft attempting to land in the basketball court. It was too big and it kept pinging off. All of a sudden, a blinding light filled the classroom. We all covered our eyes. When we looked back outside, the basketball hoops were gone.

When the doors opened, two slimy, blue aliens came out and, guess what? The aliens were staring at me. The one that looked old pointed at me and marched into the school's front door. Everyone stared at me. Then, I saw the spaceship tear a gigantic hole in the roof.

Suddenly, people in my class started disappearing. They even took my teacher! I quickly sprinted to Holly Class. It was happening in there too. In fact, there was a fleet abducting everyone from each class.

Suddenly, my heart stopped. I saw the rotten aliens lifting Megan into the air. Megan is my best friend in the whole, wide world!

I ran to her and used all my strength and rage in my body to pull her down. I think I pulled too hard though because I pulled an alien out of the ship!

Caitlin Ellis (10)

White's Wood Academy, Gainsborough

Pepci's Adventure In The Woods

An extract

Dear Diary,

Guess what happened to me today? Well, let me start from the beginning... So, I was let out into the garden and smelled a bone. I crawled under the rickety fence so quickly, getting a scratch on my back. When I finally got out of the garden, I lost the scent of the juicy bone and got lost.

When I looked up, I saw fluffy marshmallows drifting in the sky as usual. Everything was normal except that I wasn't at home! I didn't know where I was! I just trudged around the streets until I reached the entrance to the woods. I cautiously entered the group of weeping willow trees and sat under one.

I seemed to hear the trees whispering as if they were anxious about my arrival. I heard a gentle fluttering, it sounded like a bird. I hunted for it and noticed a beautiful blackbird called Crystal. I told her my name was Pepci, then we met a cat prowling around, looking for prey. "What's your name?" we questioned the cat.

"My name's Tiger," answered the cat who then told me that, if I wanted to get back home, I'd have to face my biggest fear: mud!

The cat informed me that I had to roll in the smelly mud! I did and was able to get out of the gloomy woods. I thanked my friends gratefully and trotted off to find my house where Sophie, my owner was waiting for me patiently.

Sophie Rickett (9)
White's Wood Academy, Gainsborough

Life Of A Cat

Dear Diary,

I'm Rosie and I'm a soft, adorable kitten! In my life, I am well looked after by my lovely owners. Normally, I start my day by waking up and waiting for my owners to let me out of my room, but I had waited for an hour and I started to feel worried. I didn't know what to do, I heard nothing in the house.

I scratched the door to see if anyone heard me, but no reply. Fretting about my next move, I tried to force the door open, but failed. I guess I was stuck inside. I thought about my options, but I didn't think they would work.

After what seemed like hours (but was actually twenty minutes), I had a perfect idea - well, not perfect - but I was going to purr for help. Ten more minutes later, I heard a noise. Was it a robber coming to steal our things? I hoped not.

My heart pounded loudly. I didn't know what was going on in our house. I heard more footsteps, now getting closer to my room. They knew I was in here... Suddenly, the handle on my door turned, so I prepared to pounce on them. Just then, the door opened. Carley was behind it, not a robber! I pounced, but she caught me and cuddled me tightly.

I was home again in the love centre. I asked her where she'd been and she said, "Bed."

Carley Warwick (11)

White's Wood Academy, Gainsborough

Easter Event

Dear Diary,

Today was the day when I went to an Easter event with my family. My friends said they were going too! We got in the car and got ready to go. The engine started and then, we set off out the street, out the estate.

We were in the field and the car park was packed. We parked the car and made our way to the main part of the field. There were stalls with Easter eggs for £1. It would be dark when the fireworks display began, so there were flashing glowsticks too. Also, there were hot dogs, juice and hot drinks too.

My boots were muddy from the field as it had rained. I saw Saffron and Alesha there, so I waved to them. We found a spot where we could see the fireworks. The sun was setting and it was getting dark. A voice from the speaker said, "The fireworks will start in five, four, three, two, one!"

Then, multicoloured fireworks shot up in front of us! I could hear them shooting up and popping in the air. Some were silent and some went with a bang.

The display finished and it was roughly nine o'clock. We got back in the car and headed home.

I entered our house and went to my room and fell asleep on my bed.

Faye Levick (10)

White's Wood Academy, Gainsborough

A Day In The Life Of Doris
An extract

Dear Diary,

I woke up this morning, slightly damp and wet. I realised that I was in the field. I looked around to see my friends, Pete, Oak and Foggy, looking around like I had been. Simultaneously, we all got up and started to chase each other until Pete splashed mud on my dark, braided tail. I was just about to splash him back when Gina, Holly and Charlotte came through the gates to catch us.

It felt like minutes since Saffron brought me out yesterday, so the others and I were surprised to see them. I thought, *they'll never catch me*, as they were ten metres away. *I am the smartest and most beautiful horse in the stables. Ooh, is that a Polo?* I neighed, as I trotted the remaining distance between us.

Gina attached my lead rope and took me inside to my stable while Charlotte and Holly brought in my friends. It felt like years before Elise came to groom me. She used the body and dandy brush, plastic curry comb, rubber curry comb and of course the hoof pick.

She found all my itchy spots and freed my tail of the mud. By the time she was finished with me, I shone like the sun!

Esmé Lannigan (11)

White's Wood Academy, Gainsborough

Skye's Life

Dear Diary,

I heard that my owner was giving me up for adoption. My owner's name was Sharon. She had looked after me for three years and I would really miss her. Suddenly, I heard a noise in the kitchen, so I sprinted there and saw that she had smashed my dog bowls. I was that upset that I ran until I got to my friend's house. By that point, I was two miles from home.

As soon as I got in, I told my friend that my owner was putting me up for adoption and she said that I could live with her. About two minutes later, her owner came home and noticed that I was there. She called my owner to tell her that I was there. In the next two hours, Sharon took me to the Gainsborough adoption centre.

Over the next couple of days, I stayed at the adoption centre until a lady called Caroline and her three girls came to adopt me. That day was the best day ever because I met the next-door neighbours who also had a dog and now, we're boyfriend and girlfriend.

I can visit him whenever I want because he lives right next door. I've got two new dog bowls and I've tried new meat and new biscuits.

Gabriella Pansy Hearn (10)

White's Wood Academy, Gainsborough

My Swimming Experience!

An extract

Dear Diary,

Today was the most nerve-racking day I have ever experienced in my entire life. It was the school swimming gala and I was part of the swimming team. I'd always wanted to join the team, but I never had the courage to do so. It was all I'd ever dreamed of doing and the teacher who led the group finally accepted me.

There was one thing that worried me though. It wasn't the swimming part of it, it was the racing part. The good thing was that I knew I would be perfectly fine. I am a great swimmer! Well, that is what my friends said, so I wasn't terrified at all. I had gone through months of training anyway, improving every week we went, so that made my excitement go straight up to 100! Then, the day finally came...

Today's Saturday. On Friday, we had been through all the details, including addresses, meet-up places and many other complicated bits and bobs that were vital for us to arrive at the right place.

Luckily, we got a letter for our parents which explained everything, so I didn't need to remember anything. That was a massive relief.

Katie Andrea O'Leary (11)

White's Wood Academy, Gainsborough

My New School!

Dear Diary,

Today is my first day at my new school. I'm excited but, at the same time I'm super scared! I hope I make lots of new friends. Got to go, Mum is shouting me for breakfast!

Dear Diary,

Oh my gosh! What an amazing day I've had! Let me begin... Mum and I arrived at Primrose Primary School at around 8:30 to meet Mrs Dooley, the school's headteacher. She had thick, curly brown hair, about two foot long, with a beaming great smile that made the butterflies in my tummy disappear.

My new class is called Cherry Class, I love it! It's so bright and colourful. My new teacher is called Miss Bumblebee. She sat me next to a girl called Violet, she is so kind. She has long, blonde hair like Rapunzel.

Before we knew it, it was lunchtime Violet and I made up a dance, then I saw Miss Bumblebee next to me. "Polly, you are so good at dancing, why don't you join our after-school club dance team?"

I was super excited that my teacher wanted me to be in the dance team. I'm so happy! I had the best first day ever!

Daisy Dexter (10)

White's Wood Academy, Gainsborough

The Diary Of Me (Biscuit)

Dear Diary,

I'm a dog, a Labrador puppy and I needed a home. I needed a home where it would be warm and I could be sheltered. I knew the perfect place... the woods.

I went to the woods, it started to rain. There it was, the perfect tree. It was my only hope because I was lost, but that didn't matter because I wasn't missing from a home because I never had one. But I knew someone would find me and give me a home. I mean, who could resist a puppy like me? People always came to visit the woods and I tried to attract people to me, but I was too small for them to see. They just kept on walking. I waited for weeks until, one day, this boy came along, but he ran away in disgust.

Then, a posh girl came along in her brand new fairy costume, but she screamed. Then, a girl came along. She looked like the one. I barked, she looked back at me and squeezed me. She loved me and I loved her. We were a match! She gave me the name, Biscuit.

Hannah Louise Grimbleby (9)

White's Wood Academy, Gainsborough

Snowy's Adventure

Dear Diary,

Today, I had an amazing adventure! I had an adventure exploring Poppy's bedroom. It was the best! I will tell you more about it.

I escaped my cage by biting the door open with my sharp, white teeth. Next, I climbed out and fell onto the floor safely. I was free! I was hungry though, so I had to search for food. I first searched near the bed in a maze of teddies. It failed, so I searched near the wardrobe and there wasn't any food there either! I looked everywhere, but I couldn't find any.

I leaned against a bag of something. I was upset. Suddenly, I smelled food! It was a bag of my food! I stuffed my face full of it and ate and ate. I then climbed back into my cage and went back to sleep.

Poppy Anderton (10)
White's Wood Academy, Gainsborough

Friends

Dear Diary,

Today, I met a new person in my class and their name is Makayla Deeney. I was scared to say hello and welcome her at first, but in the end, I made friends with her. I showed her all around the school and we just really liked each other. So, that evening, I told my mum and she said, "How about you invite her for tea?"

I was so happy the next day because, when I asked her, she said yes! At break-time, we played together and I also showed her around more because she still didn't know her way around. That was how I met my best friend.

Lucie Fall (9)

White's Wood Academy, Gainsborough

Diaries Of A Gangster Hamster

Dear Diary,

Yesterday I explored the great streets of Paris and I couldn't find my way home. I got lost on the way home from the sweet shop because the sun was in my eyes and I'd left my sunglasses at home.

Because it was getting dark and I couldn't find my way, I spent the night in a motel.

In the morning, because I'd spent all my money in the sweet shop, I didn't have any money to pay for the motel so I had to sneak out without paying.

Finally, the miracle appeared and I found my way home.

Amy Elena O'Leary (10)

White's Wood Academy, Gainsborough

The Incredible Dog Walk

Dear Diary,

Today, we took our dog, Foster, for a walk. We walked him in the field for a long time. Foster loves going for walks. When we were about to leave the field, Foster wanted to stay, so he tried to run to another dog. After the field, we went to our nan's house.

When we got to our nan's, we got Foster a drink of water and we had a drink and a biscuit. Then, we said goodbye and went home. When we got home, we let Foster have a run around the garden, then he fell fast asleep in his bed.

Ella Randall (9)

White's Wood Academy, Gainsborough

Morgan Parks' Weekend

Dear Diary,

On Saturday morning, I will colour in my bedroom and read. I will play with my sisters downstairs, then I'll go out and, after I come home, I will help my mum.

On Sunday morning, I will look after my baby sister and then, I will go to my nanny's and grandad's house in the afternoon. I am happy at my nanny and grandad's house. I'm happy when I'm there, but when it's time to go, I get sad because I don't want to leave my nanny and grandad's house.

Morgan Parks (9)

White's Wood Academy, Gainsborough

My Story...

Dear Diary,

Today, I, Faith Hunt, got my karate black belt. It was amazing. Let me tell you...

So, it started with me practising my Kata, which you need to do when you start at brown belt. It went well so I had to fight with another black belt to get my black belt. I got my black belt and I went home.

When I got home, my dad and I went out because of my great work.

Faith Hunt (10)

White's Wood Academy, Gainsborough

●Young Writers®
Est. 1991

Young Writers Information

We hope you have enjoyed reading this book – and that you will continue to in the coming years.

If you're a young writer who enjoys reading and creative writing, or the parent of an enthusiastic poet or story writer, do visit our website **www.youngwriters.co.uk**. Here you will find free competitions, workshops and games, as well as recommended reads, a poetry glossary and our blog. There's lots to keep budding writers motivated to write!

If you would like to order further copies of this book, or any of our other titles, then please give us a call or order via your online account.

Young Writers
Remus House
Coltsfoot Drive
Peterborough
PE2 9BF
(01733) 890066
info@youngwriters.co.uk

Join in the conversation!
Tips, news, giveaways and much more!

 **YoungWritersUK**   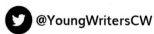 **@YoungWritersCW**